The story of *Chicken Licken* has been passed down for generations. There are many versions of the story. The following tale is a retelling of the original version. While the story has been cut for length and level, the basic elements of the classic tale remain.

One day, an acorn fell and hit Chicken Licken on the head.

"Oh my!" she cried. "The sky is falling down!
I must go and tell the king."

Along the way, Chicken Licken met
Henny Penny.

"Where are you going in such a hurry?"
asked Henny Penny.

“The sky is falling down!” cried Chicken Licken.

“We must go and tell the king! Follow me!”

Soon they met Cocky Locky.

“Where are you two going in such a hurry?” asked Cocky Locky.

“The sky is falling down!” cried Chicken Licken.
“We must go and tell the king! Follow us!”

Then they met Ducky Lucky.

"Where are you all going in such a hurry?" asked Ducky Lucky.

"The sky is falling down! We must go and tell the king!" cried Chicken Licken. "Follow us!"

Later they met Goosey Loosey.

"Where are you all going in such a hurry?" asked Goosey Loosey.

“The sky is falling down! We must go and tell the king!” cried Chicken Licken. “Follow us!”

Then they met Turkey Lurkey.

"Where are you all going in such a hurry?" asked Turkey Lurkey.

“The sky is falling down! We must go and tell the king!” cried Chicken Licken. “Follow us!”

So Chicken Licken, Henny Penny, Cocky Locky, Ducky Lucky, Goosey Loosey, and Turkey Lurkey hurried off to tell the king the sky was falling down.

They were well on their way when they met Foxy Loxy.

"Where are you all going in such a hurry?" snarled Foxy Loxy.

They all cried, "The sky is falling down!
We must go and tell the king!"

"Oh no! You are going in the wrong direction," said Foxy Loxy. "Follow me. I'll show you the way."

Chicken Little, Henny Penny, Cocky Locky, Ducky Lucky, Goosey Loosey, and Turkey Lurkey followed Foxy Loxy deep into the forest.

In fact, they followed Foxy Loxy
right into his cave!

Chicken Little, Henny Penny, Cocky Locky, Ducky Lucky, Goosey Loosey, and Turkey Lurkey have not been seen since that day.

And the king never did hear that the sky was falling down.

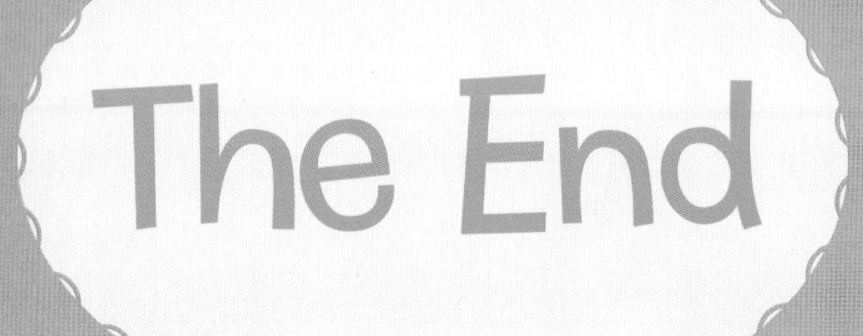
The End